Royce Sarpy

& the Twin Day Disaster

By Royce Sinclair Sarpy, M.Ed.
Illustrated By Cameron Wilson

Table of Contents

Chapter one
The Twins

The twins did everything together. They played the same sports, rapped the same songs, and did the same dances. They even brushed their teeth together.

Royce shared a room with the twins. There was just enough space for the three of them. They had two of everything, so he made sure to keep his things very neat. He slept in the bed across from Quincy and Quinton's bunkbed.

"Man, I wish I could sleep in the castle beds," Royce said to himself.

"Are you ready for your first day of school, grape head?" Quinton asked Royce.

"He's probably scared," Quincy teased. Royce wondered what it would be like to not have these two around.

"I'll be fine. I have your teacher from last year, Quinton. This should be easy as one-two-three."

"Boys, it's time for bed. You all have to be well rested for your first day of school tomorrow," Mama called.

Chapter two
first day jitters

It was the morning of the first day of school. Everyone in the family was getting ready. Quincy took some shirts from the hamper. "You can have these. I wore it my first day of school last year," he said.

"That's gross!" Amber yelled. "Mama would never let you wear dirty clothes to school."

"Maybe I can ask her to wash it," Royce said nervously.

"Do you know how to tell time? We have school soon," Amber says as she walks away blasting her Walkman.

"Thanks Quincy!" Royce said. "Don't thank me. Turtles are cool, but not on a shirt," Quincy replied.

"Hey Mama could you wash this for school?" Royce said.

"I think it will be good luck, and it has the best ninja turtle." Mama was ironing Royce's clothes for the first day of school.

"Leave it in the bag, honey."

Royce frowned. "I have to wear it today!" he cried. She stopped and sat down.

"You will be just fine my chocolate drop with the curly top. You know your ABCs and 123s."

Royce sighed. "Well, can I bring my Buddy?" He held up his bear Granny gave him when he was a baby.

Mama hugged him. "You will make plenty of buddies at school."

Chapter three
Max and Royce

The green mini-van pulled up to the school. "Should I walk you all in?" Mama asked.

"You have the baby in the car, and I got this!" Amber said with pride.

Royce stared at the huge glass doors in amazement. Amber and the twins wished him luck and went their separate ways.

"Wait, I don't think I'm ready!" said Royce. There, he stood alone in a long hallway filled with doors.

"Hi, I'm Max! Kindergarten is this way."

Royce was still silent. He had only two friends, Quincy and Quinton, so this was new to him.

"Hello, dude?" Max waved his hand. "Do you know which class you have?" Max said. Royce was still silent.

"Fine, come on!" Max took Royce's hand and they walked to Ms. Smith's classroom.

"This guy is lost!"
Max said sharply.

He looked at Ms. Smith
happily. "You look like
my mom," Royce said.

"You are a Sarpy! You
look so much like your
brother. Come on in!"
said Ms. Smith.

Chapter Four
Turtle Power

"When is lunch?" said Max. "We do not call out in school, and we have lunch at noon," Ms. Smith replied.

Max sunk into his seat.

"She is mean," he whispered. "Hey, what did you bring for lunch?" Royce stayed focused on making shapes.

"Class line up." Ms. Smith called. They transitioned to the cafeteria. "Wow look at all these tables and people," Royce said to himself.

Suddenly, Quincy and Quinton ran up. "New friend? How's your day smarty?" they said.

Royce quickly answered, "Yes, this is Max! He's in my class. We are going to eat together. They walked to their lunch table.

"Wow, you can talk," Max said with a smirk.

The boys sat down and enjoyed their lunch. Max had school lunch. Royce had a home cooked burger, fries, and a fruit cup. "I'm Royce. I apologize for not talking toyou." "It's fine. You can repay me with some of those fries!" Max said.

"What do you watch on T.V.?" "I don't have cable, so just ninja turtles and stuff." Max slammed down his fork.

"Dude, I love ninja turtles!" Royce's eyes grew bigger.

"I actually have two ninja turtle shirts. It's one of the good things about having twin brothers in first grade." Max stood up. "Let's have a twin day tomorrow!" he shouted. Max wasn't so bad after all.

Chapter Five
Sneaky Swap

"Hey Mama, did you get a chance to wash those shirts?" Royce asked. Mama was busy making everyone breakfast, packing lunch, snacks, and nursing the baby.

"Check the clothesline, honey, and be sure to put one away," Mama said.

"I know. I have to take care of them so I can give the handy down to the little one," Royce said.

"For the last time, they are called hand-me-downs!"

"Handy makes sense because they come in handy," he said softly. As he got dressed, he made sure to hide the other shirt in his backpack instead.

That day at school it was almost time for lunch. "I have to use the restroom," said Royce. Max was already waiting in the restroom to switch shirts.

"One boy at a time," said Ms. Smith.

"It's an emergency!" Royce cried.

"This time only," Ms. Smith replied.

Royce had the other shirt stuffed under the one he was wearing. "You look a little full today, young man," said Ms. Smith.

"Uhh...I had a big breakfast?" Royce said.

As he scratched his head, the shirt fell to the carpet. "This is an emergency. You have shirts falling from your belly!" Ms. Smith said sharply.
He dropped his head.

That night at home, Mama had a long talk with Royce. "Honey, wanting a friend should not make you change who you are." Royce looked down in shame.

"I am raising you to be honest, and your friends should be too. Anyone who wants you to lie is not a friend."

"It wasn't Max who lied. It was me," Royce cried. Mama looked shocked as she listened.

"I know it was wrong. I just got really excited about having a buddy. I apologize for not being honest," he said.

"I know son, but you don't need to lie to have a buddy. You just need to be you." Mama winked.

"Well, true because I'm always honest with you, and you're my best buddy other than Buddy of course."

Mama hugged him tight until she heard the baby crying. "Oh, let's see what has Sessle fussing," she said.

CPSIA information can be obtained
at www.ICGtesting.com
Printed in the USA
BVHW021420101220
595355BV00057B/273